Rosa and Fredo

SUPa DOOPERS

sundance   Newbridge®

Rosa and Fredo

sundance **Newbridge**

Copyright © 1999 Sundance Newbridge Publishing

Published by
Sundance Newbridge Publishing
33 Boston Post Road West
Suite 440
Marlborough, MA 01752
800-343-8204
SundanceNewbridge.com

Copyright © text Jim Howes
Copyright © illustrations Ian Forss
Project commissioned and managed by
Lorraine Bambrough-Kelly, The Writer's Style
Designed by Cath Lindsey/design rescue

First published 1997 by
Addison Wesley Longman Australia Pty Limited
95 Coventry Street
South Melbourne 3205 Australia
Exclusive United States Distribution: Sundance Newbridge Publishing

ISBN 978-0-7608-1922-7

Printed by Nordica International Ltd.
Manufactured in Guangzhou, China
September, 2018
Nordica Job#: CA21801126
SunNew PO#: 229166

CONTENTS

CHAPTER 1

Off to the Market

"It's time to take the fruit and vegetables to the market," said Rosa's mother.

So Rosa, who almost always did what grown-ups told her, loaded the baskets onto their donkey, Fredo. Then she put the fruit and vegetables into the baskets. "I'm ready," she called.

Her mother came out and checked the load. "Be sure to go straight to the market," she said.

Rosa and Fredo started down the dusty
path that led to the town and the market.
They had lots of fresh fruit and vegetables
to carry, and the load made Fredo walk
slowly.

Rosa stopped at the creek to let him drink
and to have a small snack of the flowers
that grew nearby.

When it was time to go, Rosa called to Fredo to get moving. But Fredo was feeling lazy and had fallen asleep under a tree.

Rosa poked him with her finger. But Fredo simply shifted a little and went back to sleep.

"Come on, Fredo," pleaded Rosa. "We have to get to the market before noon, or it will be too late to sell our fruit and vegetables."

But Fredo was not ready to move and simply snored a bit louder.

CHAPTER 2

What Will She Do?

Rosa was wondering what to do when she saw a man coming along the path. He had a donkey with him, too, and seemed to be talking to it as they walked.

"That's it, Miguel," Rosa heard the man say. "Good donkey. Have some more fruit." As they walked, the man was feeding the donkey from the baskets. When they reached Rosa and Fredo, they stopped.

"Good morning, neighbor," said the man. Rosa noticed that he was very thin and that his donkey was about as twice as wide as Fredo.

"Are you in trouble?" he asked.

"We stopped here for a little rest and a snack on our way to the market, and now I can't get my donkey to move," explained Rosa.

"If we don't get to the market soon, nobody will be left to buy our fruit and vegetables."

"I can help you," said the man. "To get your donkey to move, all you have to do is show it some kindness." As he spoke, he fed another couple of apples to his own donkey.

"Just feed your animal well and talk to it in a friendly way, and it will do what you want."

With that, the man and his donkey wandered slowly down the path.

After he had gone, Rosa, who almost always did what grown-ups told her, took some fruit from one of the baskets and held it out to Fredo. "Come on, Fredo, there's a good donkey. We have to get to the market."

The donkey opened its eyes, sniffed the apple, ate it, licked its lips, and closed its eyes again. Rosa tried again, this time with a carrot. Once again, Fredo ate what Rosa offered and went back to sleep.

Six times Rosa tried to get Fredo up and going by feeding him and talking in a friendly way. Six times Fredo ate the food and went back to sleep.

CHAPTER 3

Cracking the Whip

Rosa was getting very worried. She sat down on the rock again and put her head in her hands.

She looked up when she heard a noise from down the path.

There was another man coming along the road with his donkey. The donkey was very thin and had a worried look on its face. The man looked very serious and carried a long thin stick with a leather whip on the end.

Every time the donkey slowed down, the man cracked the whip and shouted, "Faster, you lazy animal, or there's no food for you when we get to the market!" Then the donkey would speed up again.

They stopped when they came to where Rosa was sitting. "Good morning, neighbor," said the man. "Are you in some kind of trouble?"

Rosa explained, "We stopped here for a rest, and now my donkey refuses to move. I have fed him all sorts of treats from the baskets, but it makes no difference. Now I am afraid we will never reach the market in time to sell our fruit and vegetables."

"I can help you," said the man. "The way to handle a donkey is simple. Just show it who is the boss." With that, he cracked his whip right next to his donkey's ears. It stopped drinking and set off down the path. "See?" yelled the man.

After they had gone, Rosa, who almost
always did what grown-ups told her, looked
around for a long thin branch. She found
one that was long and thin like a whip.
Stepping up next to Fredo, she whisked the
branch over his head. It made a sound like
the wind through a hole in a wall.

Rosa flicked the stick back over her head and whipped it forward so fast that it let out a loud CRACK! just over Fredo's ears.

The donkey was so startled, it sat up with a bolt and ran around in circles. Fruit and vegetables scattered everywhere.

Rosa ran behind Fredo, trying to catch the animal. When she finally caught up with him, Fredo had scattered the load all over the ground.

It took Rosa a long time to soothe Fredo and load everything back into the baskets again.

CHAPTER 4

Rosa's Bright Idea

After all that running around, both Rosa and Fredo needed a rest.

While they were sitting next to the creek, Rosa looked at the stick on the ground. Then she looked at the big carrot sticking out of the basket. And then she had an idea.

She took the big carrot and picked up the stick. "Now, all I need is some string," she said, as she dug into her pockets.

With those three things, Rosa worked out how to get her load to the market.

On her way, she passed the man who had showed her how he used a whip to make his donkey work. They had stopped because the donkey had become so frightened that it had climbed a tree.

"Please come down," the man was saying. "I promise not to frighten you any more." But the donkey looked like it would never come down.

Rosa smiled politely and waved as she went past with Fredo. "See, I used the stick like you told me," she called.

Further along, she came to the man who had told her to pamper Fredo to get him moving. The man was still moving, but now *he* was the one carrying the load. And he was carrying something else — his donkey! The man was puffing and panting like he might burst.

Rosa smiled politely and waved as she went past with Fredo. "See, I used the food like you told me," she called.

When Rosa returned home, her mother asked her about the trip. "Did you have any trouble?" she asked. "Sometimes Fredo can be a bit stubborn."

"Oh, not really," said Rosa. "I did have a small problem with him, but I managed to solve it."

"Did you meet any people on your way?" asked Rosa's mother.

"Yes," said Rosa. "They told me how to keep Fredo moving."

"And did their advice help you?"

Rosa thought for a moment before answering. "Yes, as a matter of fact, it did."

"That's wonderful, dear," said her mother. "I'm so glad you're one of those good children who always does what grown-ups tell her to do."

"Always," said Rosa with a smile.

ABOUT THE AUTHOR

Jim Howes

Jim Howes writes children's books, works on magazines, and was a member of the team that created *Lift Off,* an Australian TV show. *Rosa and Fredo* is the fortieth book that he has written for children. His next book, *Set Me Free,* is a novel. It is scheduled to be published soon.

About the Illustrator

Ian Forss

In 1969, when Ian Forss was nine years old, his mother commented that a picture he had drawn looked "nice." That was all the encouragement he needed. From then on, he was always to be found drawing pictures.

Ian drew all the way through college as he earned a degree in Art and Design. And when he went on to earn a graduate degree in Film and Television, he was still drawing.

Today, Ian lives with his wife, Linda, and two children, Jade and James. He enjoys riding his horse, Apache, even if sometimes it makes drawing steady lines a bit tricky.